The Talent Show

Story by Alan Trussell-Cullen

Illustrations by Elise Hurst

Contents

Chapter 1   Abby's Partner   2

Chapter 2   Teamwork   8

Chapter 3   Magic!   14

Chapter 4   The Incredible Vanishing Act   18

Rigby®

HOUGHTON MIFFLIN HARCOURT
Supplemental Publishers

www.Rigby.com
800-531-5015

Chapter 1

Abby's Partner

It was nearly the end of the year.

"Today we're going to start getting ready for our talent show," said Mrs. James. "We're going to work in pairs, and each pair will prepare an act for the show."

The children were excited, including Abby and Zoe. Abby and Zoe were identical twins. They couldn't wait to find out who their partners would be.

"There's only one person I don't want to have as my partner," Abby whispered to Zoe.

"I know who that is—Joel Bradford!" Zoe whispered to Abby.

Abby nodded and said, "He's such a show-off!"

Zoe's partner turned out to be Max.

"You're lucky!" Abby whispered to Zoe. "Max can play the piano, so you'll be able to do something musical."

Abby put her hand into the hat and pulled out a piece of paper.

"Joel!" she read out loud.

"Hi, Abby," said Joel, grinning. "Welcome to my team!"

Abby just smiled.

The next day, Zoe and Max decided they would do a duet. It was a song that Max already knew how to play on the piano. Zoe just had to learn the words, but she knew it wouldn't take her long to know them by heart.

All of the other children quickly started working, too. Everyone knew what they were going to do—everyone except Abby and Joel.

Chapter 2

Teamwork

"I know!" said Joel. "I can do a juggling act and you can be my assistant!"

"That sounds all right," said Abby. "Can you juggle?"

"I've never tried," said Joel. "But it can't be too hard."

He picked up two pencil bags and began to throw them in the air. One landed on Mrs. James's desk and the other almost went through the window.

"Some juggler!" said Abby.

"I know!" said Joel. "I'll be a clown!"

"Can you tell a joke?" asked Abby.

"I can't think of any," replied Joel.

"Some clown!" said Abby. Then she had an idea. "Let's ask Mrs. James for help," she suggested.

"A good act requires teamwork," said Mrs. James. "You need to use what you are both good at."

"I'm good at talking," said Joel.

"Everyone knows that," said Abby. "But it doesn't help with our act, does it? It's going to take magic to get us to work together."

"Maybe that's your answer," said Mrs. James.

Abby looked at Joel and Joel looked at Abby. "Yes!" they said.

Chapter 3

Magic!

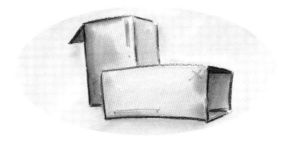

"A magic act!" said Abby. "We'll need two big boxes."

"My dad works for a store that sells refrigerators," said Joel. "I'll get two big refrigerator boxes. We can paint them and put curtains in front."

"Good thinking, Joel!" said Abby. "I'll ask Mom if she has any old curtains we can use."

"Sounds like good teamwork," said Mrs. James.

During the next few days, Abby and Joel were busy getting their act ready. Zoe and Max already knew their song, so Zoe helped Abby, too.

The night of the talent show arrived, and everyone was very excited. Mrs. James spoke to the parents first, and then the curtains opened and the show began.

Zoe and Max were on early. Their song went well and the audience clapped.

Chapter 4
The Incredible Vanishing Act

Abby and Joel's act was the last one in the talent show. When the curtains opened, there was Joel the magician and Abby his assistant. Behind them were two huge boxes with curtains hanging in front.

"Ladies and gentlemen," said Joel. "I'm the famous magician Joel and this is Abby, my amazing assistant! Tonight we will perform an incredible vanishing act. First I will ask my amazing assistant to enter this magical box."

Abby stepped into the box and closed the curtain.

"I will now say the magic word," said Joel. "Abracadabra!" Then Joel pulled back the curtain. The box was empty!

"Where has my amazing assistant gone?" asked Joel.

"Try the other box!" someone in the audience shouted.

"Aha!" said Joel, and he pulled back the curtain on the other box.

Out jumped his amazing assistant!

The audience was delighted and started clapping. They were still clapping as the curtain closed.

"Joel, that was incredible!" said Mrs. James as she came backstage. "How did you do it?"

"Ask my amazing assistant," said Joel.

"Teamwork!" said the amazing assistant. "Look in here, Mrs. James. In this first box is a secret door. Knock on it!"

Mrs. James knocked on the secret door and it opened. Out jumped another amazing assistant! Both amazing assistants were dressed exactly the same and they looked exactly alike.

Mrs. James laughed and said, "Two amazing assistants! What a smart trick. But which one is Abby, and which one is Zoe?"

"That's easy!" said Joel. "This one is Abby, and this one is Zoe!"

"Almost right!" said Abby, laughing. Then she put one arm around Zoe's shoulder and the other around Joel's. "But you'll never guess what we learned, Mrs. James," she said.

"What was that?" asked Mrs. James.

"Teamwork works!" said Abby.

"Yes," said Zoe. "Like magic!"